Bye, Mis' Lela

DOROTHY CARTER

PICTURES BY

HARVEY STEVENSON

FRANCES FOSTER BOOKS

FARRAR, STRAUS AND GIROUX

NEW YORK

Mis' Lela was my mama's friend.
When Mama went to work I stayed
with her.
Sometimes I cried.
I didn't want Mama to leave me.
Mis' Lela said, "Come 'ere, Sugar
Plum, and sit on Mis' Lela's lap.
I'm gonna wipe those dewdrops
off your cheeks."

She gave me pancakes and coffee
milk for breakfast.

Carrie and Jerry and L.C. and all
the children goin' to school waved
at us and said, "Hi, Mis' Lela. Hi,
Lil Sugar."
Mis' Lela waved back and said,
"Study your lessons and mind
your manners, children."
"Yes, ma'am, Mis' Lela, bye,"
they said.

I played in her yard with her chickens, geese, and billy goat.

'Long came Mr. Tinker Man, dragging pots, pans, buckets, and dippers.

They dangled and clattered over his back.

"He's gonna mend one hole and punch two, making more leaks in my tin tubs," Mis' Lela grumbled.

I banged his pots with my drumstick.

When I got all dirtied up, Mis'
Lela put me in her washtub.
"You'll be sweet-smelling when
your mama comes for you."
I splashed around in the water till
the dirt was off me, and I dried
myself.
Then I put on my clean overalls.

And 'long came Mis' Bible Lady
in her car, clonking and honking.
She brought red-and-gold books
showing pictures of kings, angels,
and devils.
I leaned on Mis' Lela's lap and
looked at the pictures while the
Bible Lady talked a lot.
She said the Comforter was
coming soon.
"My, that woman can talk,"
said Mis' Lela.

"Now lie down on that cot and
go to sleep, Little Bit.
Mis' Lela got to get back to
bustin' suds," she said.
She gave me ginger cake.

When I woke up, Mama was sitting
on the steps waiting to take me
home.

"Say, Bye, Mis' Lela, and give her
a hug," Mama said.
Mis' Lela wrapped me in her arms.
She smelled like soapsuds and
ginger cake.

And then one day Mis' Lela died.
Mama took me to her wake.
People from everywhere were
there, standin' roun', bent over
in her yard.
Carrie, Jerry, L.C., and all the
children sat bunched together—
bein' still on the front porch.

People stood in the dining room
and parlor.
Mr. Tinker Man and Mis' Bible
Lady opened the baskets of food.
They spread it in heaps on the
long kitchen table where me and
Mis' Lela ate together.

The grown folks and Miss Bible
Lady talked low 'bout Miss Lela
restin' with the Comforter.
They ate supper at Mis' Lela's
table.
The Tinker Man and the children
ate on the front porch.
I didn't want to eat.
Mama said, "I'll just take a little
somethin' home with me."
But she didn't.

Mis' Lela was dressed up in her
Sunday-go-to-meeting clothes,
sleeping in her bed.

"Say, Bye, Mis' Lela," Mama
whispered.
"Can she hear me?" I asked.
"Dead people can't hear, child,"
Mama said.
"Can she see me?" I asked.
"She can't see, either," Mama said.

"Can she eat?" I kept askin'.
Mama shook her head.
"Is Mis' Lela sleeping, Mama?"
I asked.
"Yeah—it's a long, long sleep,
child," Mama said.
"Can she dream?" I asked Mama.
"No more dreaming.
No more toiling.
Say, Bye, Mis' Lela," Mama said.
I shut my eyes tight.

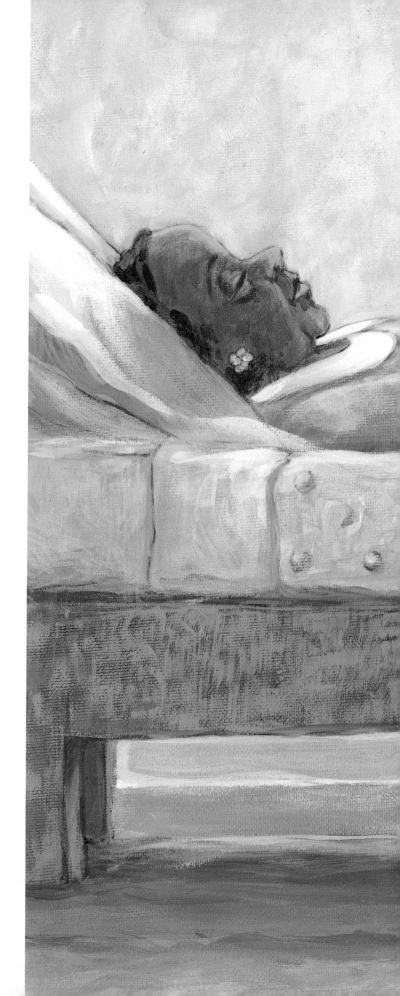

Mama held my hand and we
walked home in the dark.
That night, Mama let me sleep
with her.

For a long time I dreamed and
dreamed Mis' Lela was still taking
care of me.
But she wasn't.

After that, Mama took me to
the bakery with her.
She cooked cakes iced on top
with chocolate and coconut.
"Here's the bowl," Mama said,
hurrying 'round.
I scraped the bowl clean and
made a cupcake.
Mama made pies, too—custard
and blackberry.
She gave the trimmings to me.
I rolled the dough and made a
berry pie.
Mama smiled.
"You're a smart helper," she said.
"Now let's cool off."
We drank cold lemonade.

I grew bigger and went to school.
When I walked by Mis' Lela's
house, I said, "Hi," same as she
was there sayin' to me, "Study
your lessons, Sugar Plum, and
mind your manners."
I said, "Yes, ma'am. Bye, Mis' Lela."

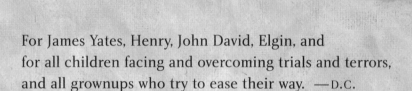

For James Yates, Henry, John David, Elgin, and
for all children facing and overcoming trials and terrors,
and all grownups who try to ease their way. —D.C.

For Frances —H.S.

Text copyright © 1998 by Dorothy Carter
Pictures copyright © 1998 by Harvey Stevenson
All rights reserved
Distributed in Canada by Douglas & McIntyre Ltd.
Color separations by Hong Kong Scanner Arts
Printed and bound in the United States of America by Berryville Graphics
Designed by Filomena Tuosto
First edition, 1998

Library of Congress Cataloging-in-Publication Data
Carter, Dorothy (Dorothy A.)
    Bye, Mis' Lela / Dorothy Carter ; pictures by Harvey Stevenson.—
1st ed.
        p.   cm.
    "A Frances Foster book."
    Summary: At first, Sugar Plum cries when her mother leaves her with Mis' Lela, but the happy days they
spend together make Sugar Plum want to remember her, even after she dies.
    ISBN 0-374-31013-0
    [1. Babsitters—Fiction. 2. Death—Fiction. 3. Afro-Americans—Fiction.] I. Stevenson, Harvey, ill. II. Title.
PZ7.C2433By   1997
[E]—DC20   95-33516